# TEENAGE MUTANT NINJA TURTLES

## LEONARDO

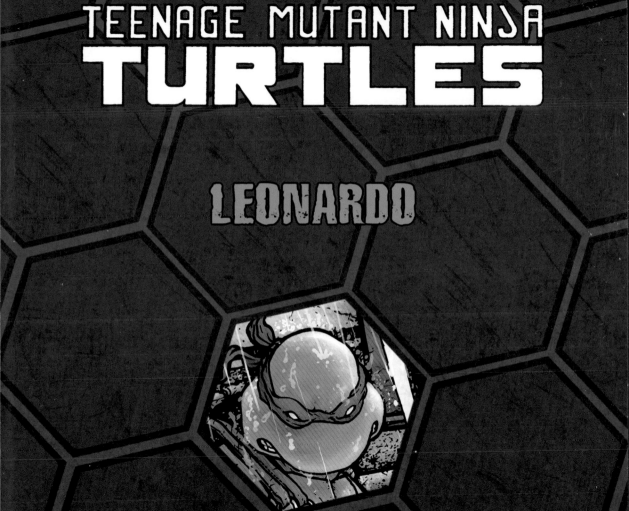

**ABDOPUBLISHING.COM**

Reinforced library bound edition published in 2015 by Spotlight,
a division of ABDO, PO Box 398166, Minneapolis, Minnesota 55439.
Spotlight produces high-quality reinforced library bound editions for
schools and libraries. Published by agreement with IDW.

Printed in the United States of America, North Mankato, Minnesota.
112014
012015

 THIS BOOK CONTAINS
RECYCLED MATERIALS

**LIBRARY OF CONGRESS CATALOGING-IN-PUBLICATION DATA**

Lynch, Brian (Brian Michael), 1973-
  Leonardo / writer, Brian Lynch ; artist, Ross Campbell. -- Reinforced library
bound edition.
     pages cm. --  (Teenage Mutant Ninja Turtles)
  Summary: "Leonardo does battle with the ruthless Foot Clan"-- Provided
by publisher.
  ISBN 978-1-61479-339-7
1.  Graphic novels.  I. Campbell, Ross, 1979- illustrator. II. Teenage Mutant
Ninja Turtles (Television program : 2012- ) III. Title.
  PZ7.7.L95Le 2015
  741.5'973--dc23

                    2014038216

**Spotlight**

A Division of ABDO
abdopublishing.com

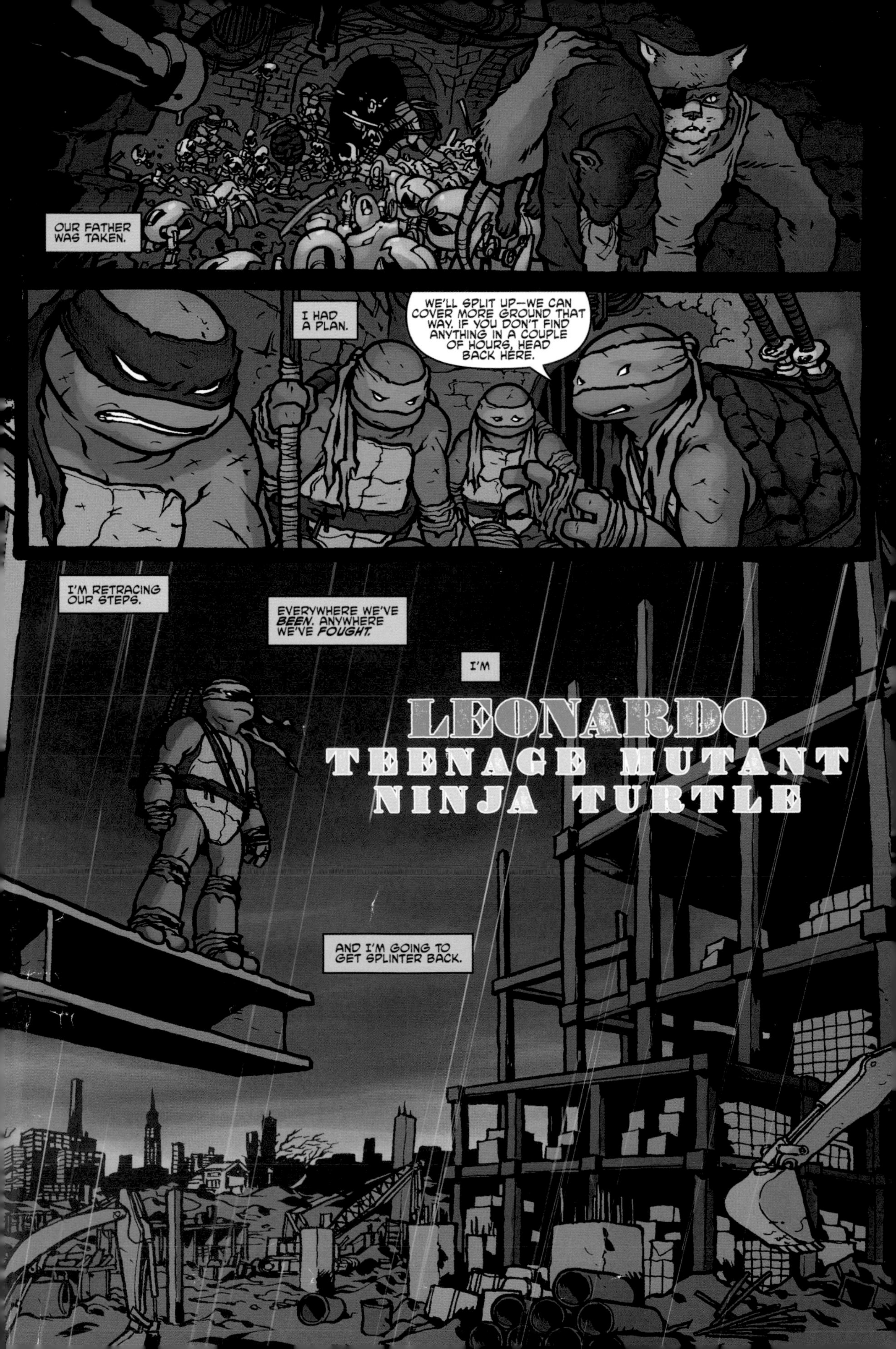
OUR FATHER WAS TAKEN.
I HAD A PLAN.
WE'LL SPLIT UP—WE CAN COVER MORE GROUND THAT WAY. IF YOU DON'T FIND ANYTHING IN A COUPLE OF HOURS, HEAD BACK HERE.
I'M RETRACING OUR STEPS.
EVERYWHERE WE'VE BEEN. ANYWHERE WE'VE FOUGHT.
I'M
LEONARDO
TEENAGE MUTANT NINJA TURTLE
AND I'M GOING TO GET SPLINTER BACK.

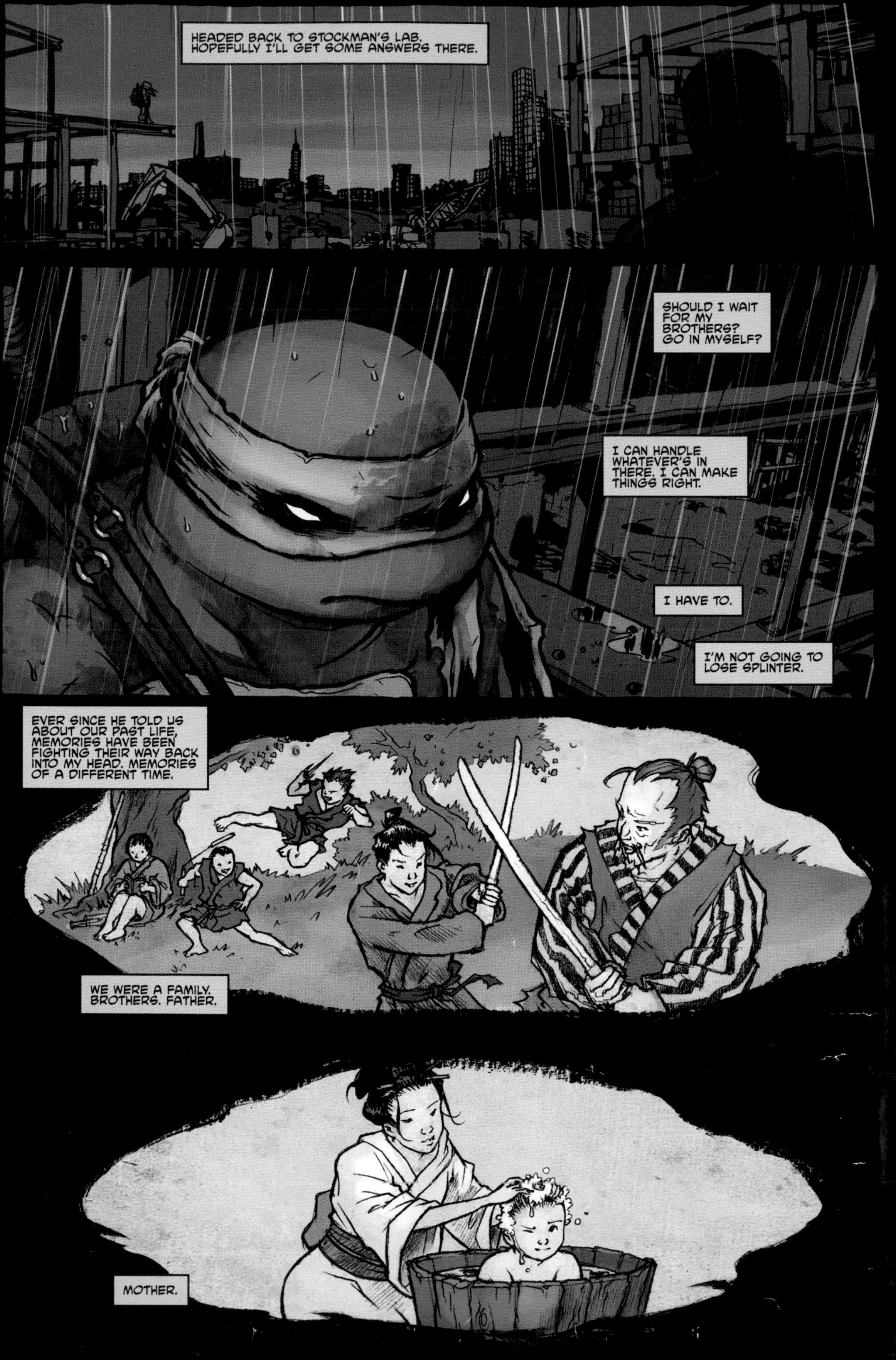
HEADED BACK TO STOCKMAN'S LAB. HOPEFULLY I'LL GET SOME ANSWERS THERE.
SHOULD I WAIT FOR MY BROTHERS? GO IN MYSELF?
I CAN HANDLE WHATEVER'S IN THERE. I CAN MAKE THINGS RIGHT.
I HAVE TO.
I'M NOT GOING TO LOSE SPLINTER.
EVER SINCE HE TOLD US ABOUT OUR PAST LIFE, MEMORIES HAVE BEEN FIGHTING THEIR WAY BACK INTO MY HEAD. MEMORIES OF A DIFFERENT TIME.
WE WERE A FAMILY. BROTHERS. FATHER.
MOTHER.

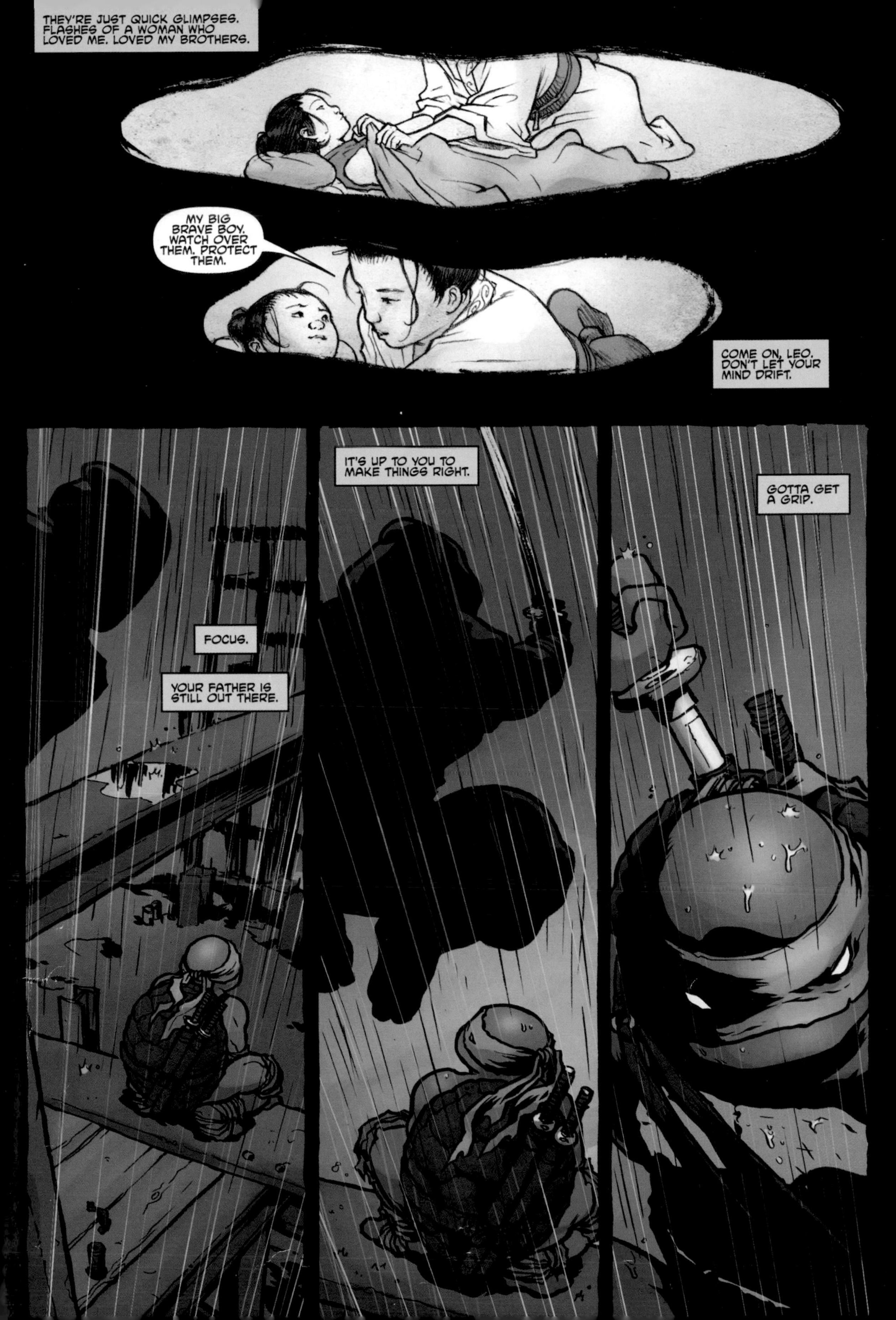
THEY'RE JUST QUICK GLIMPSES. FLASHES OF A WOMAN WHO LOVED ME. LOVED MY BROTHERS.
MY BIG BRAVE BOY. WATCH OVER THEM. PROTECT THEM.
COME ON, LEO. DON'T LET YOUR MIND DRIFT.
FOCUS.
YOUR FATHER IS STILL OUT THERE.
IT'S UP TO YOU TO MAKE THINGS RIGHT.
GOTTA GET A GRIP.

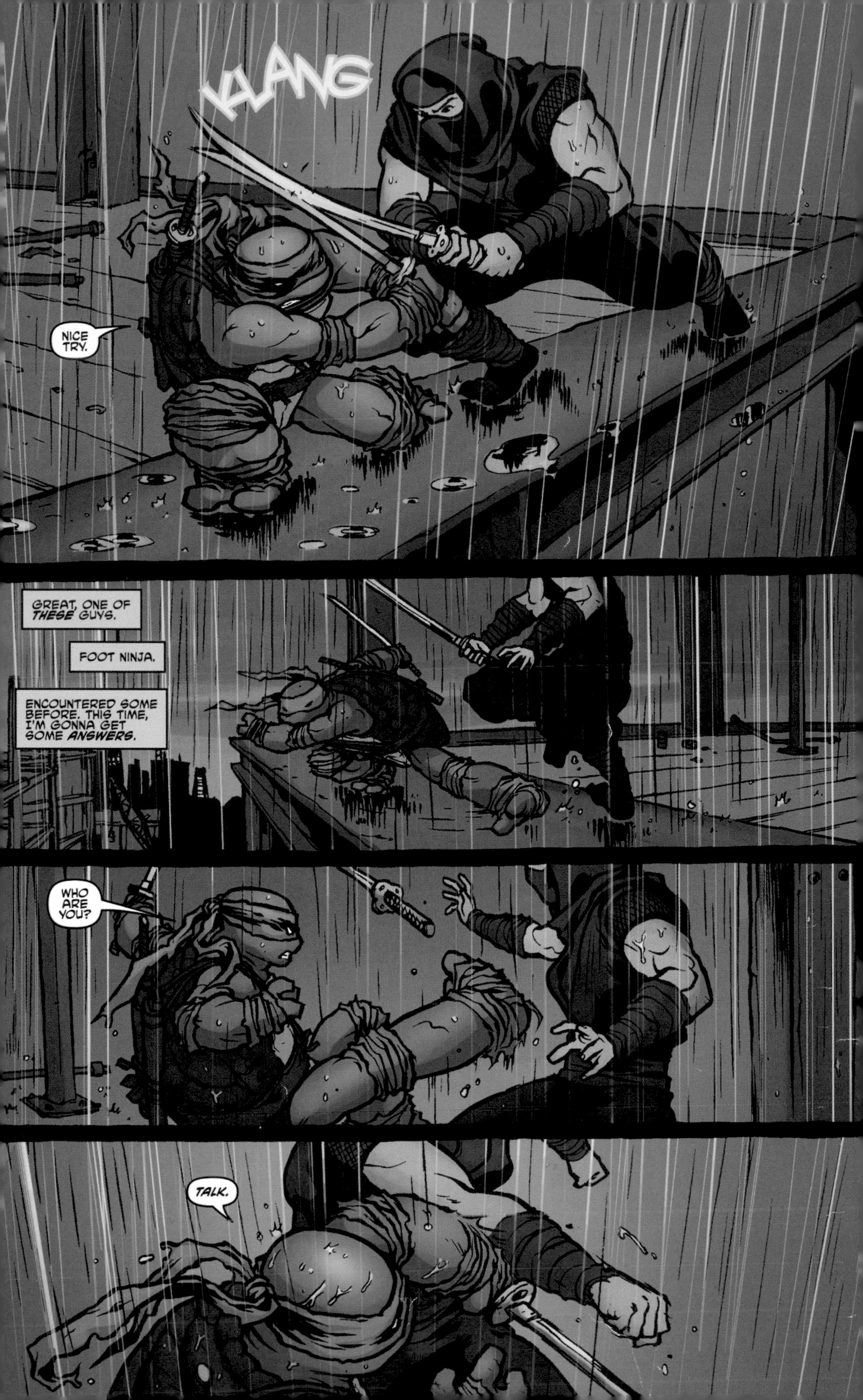
KLANG
NICE TRY.
GREAT, ONE OF *THESE* GUYS.
FOOT NINJA.
ENCOUNTERED SOME BEFORE. THIS TIME, I'M GONNA GET SOME *ANSWERS*.
WHO ARE YOU?
*TALK.*

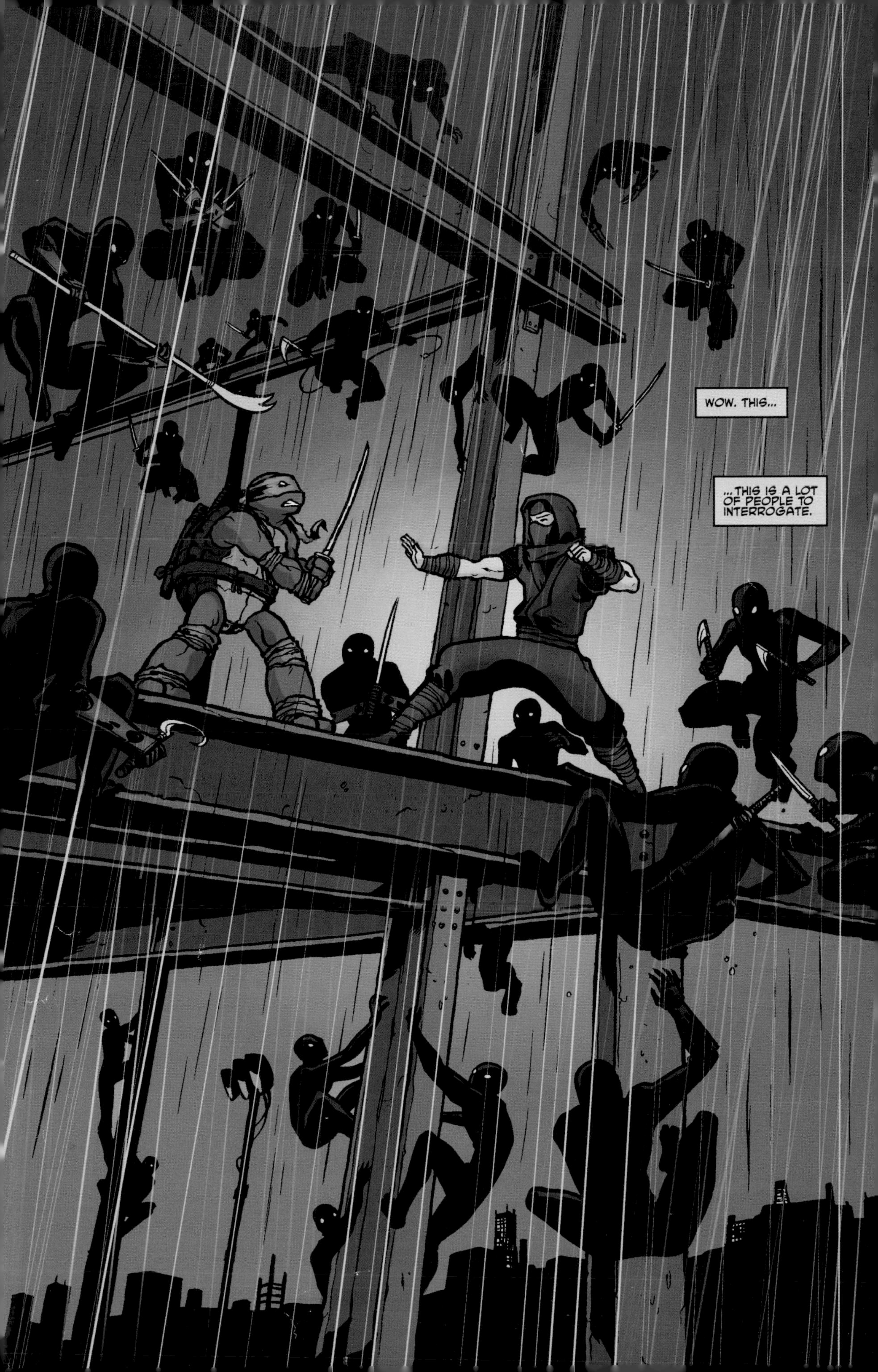
WOW. THIS...
...THIS IS A LOT OF PEOPLE TO INTERROGATE.

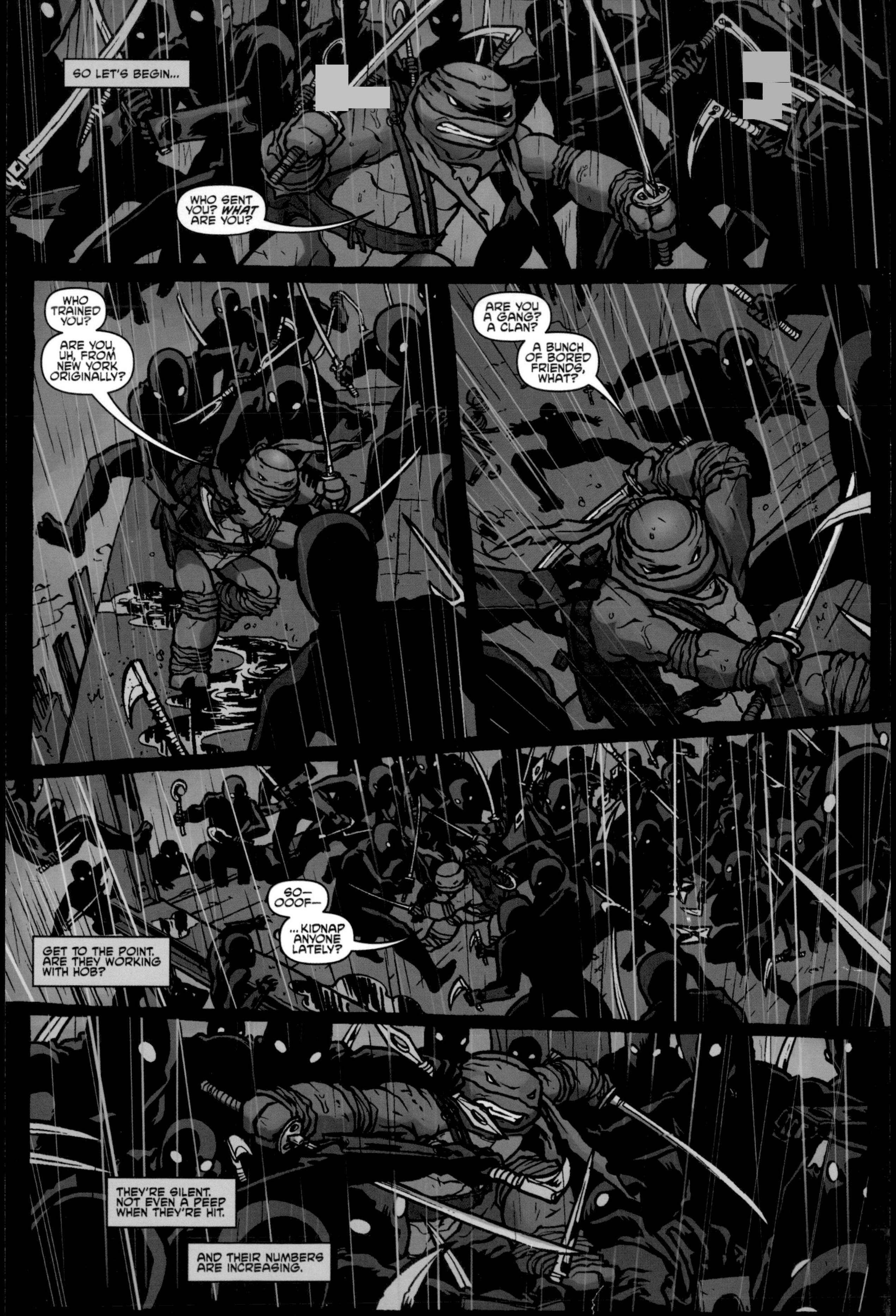
SO LET'S BEGIN...
WHO SENT YOU? *WHAT* ARE YOU?
WHO TRAINED YOU?
ARE YOU, UH, FROM NEW YORK ORIGINALLY?
ARE YOU A GANG? A CLAN?
A BUNCH OF BORED FRIENDS, WHAT?
SO—OOOF—
...KIDNAP ANYONE LATELY?
GET TO THE POINT. ARE THEY WORKING WITH HOB?
THEY'RE SILENT. NOT EVEN A PEEP WHEN THEY'RE HIT.
AND THEIR NUMBERS ARE INCREASING.

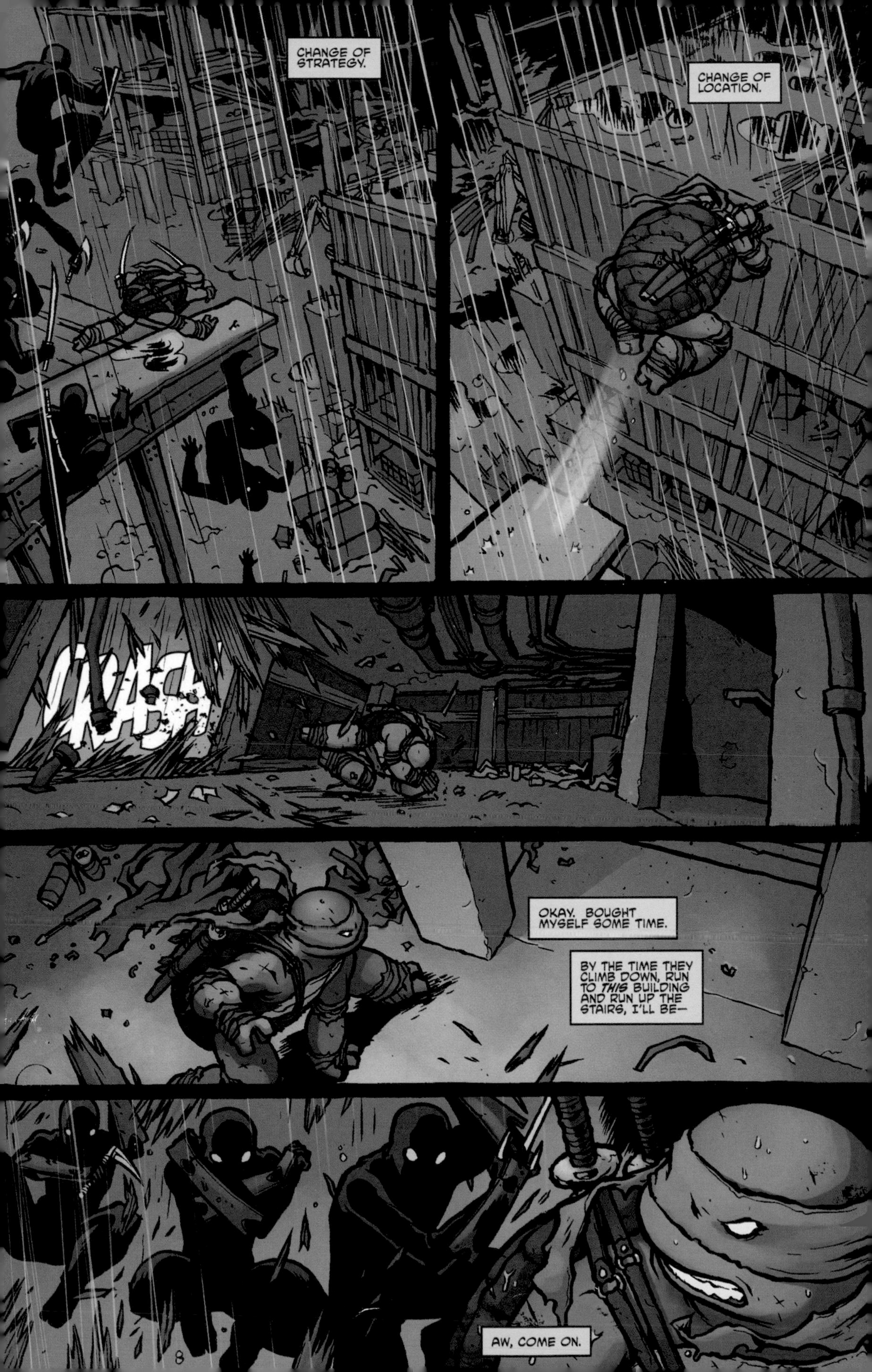

CHANGE OF STRATEGY.
CHANGE OF LOCATION.
CRASH
OKAY. BOUGHT MYSELF SOME TIME.
BY THE TIME THEY CLIMB DOWN, RUN TO *THIS* BUILDING AND RUN UP THE STAIRS, I'LL BE—
AW, COME ON.

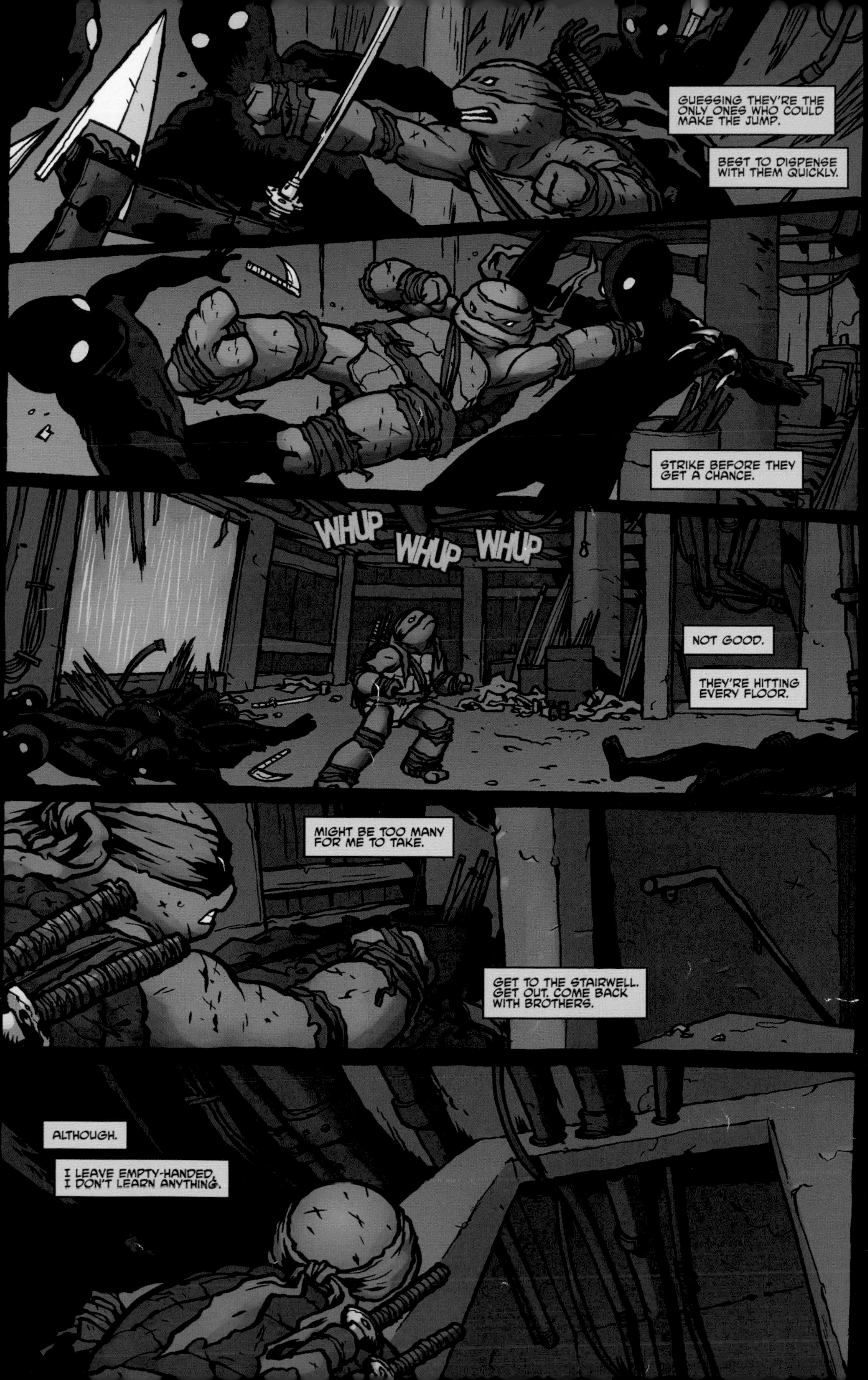
GUESSING THEY'RE THE ONLY ONES WHO COULD MAKE THE JUMP.
BEST TO DISPENSE WITH THEM QUICKLY.
STRIKE BEFORE THEY GET A CHANCE.
WHUP
WHUP
WHUP
NOT GOOD.
THEY'RE HITTING EVERY FLOOR.
MIGHT BE TOO MANY FOR ME TO TAKE.
GET TO THE STAIRWELL. GET OUT. COME BACK WITH BROTHERS.
ALTHOUGH.
I LEAVE EMPTY-HANDED, I DON'T LEARN ANYTHING.

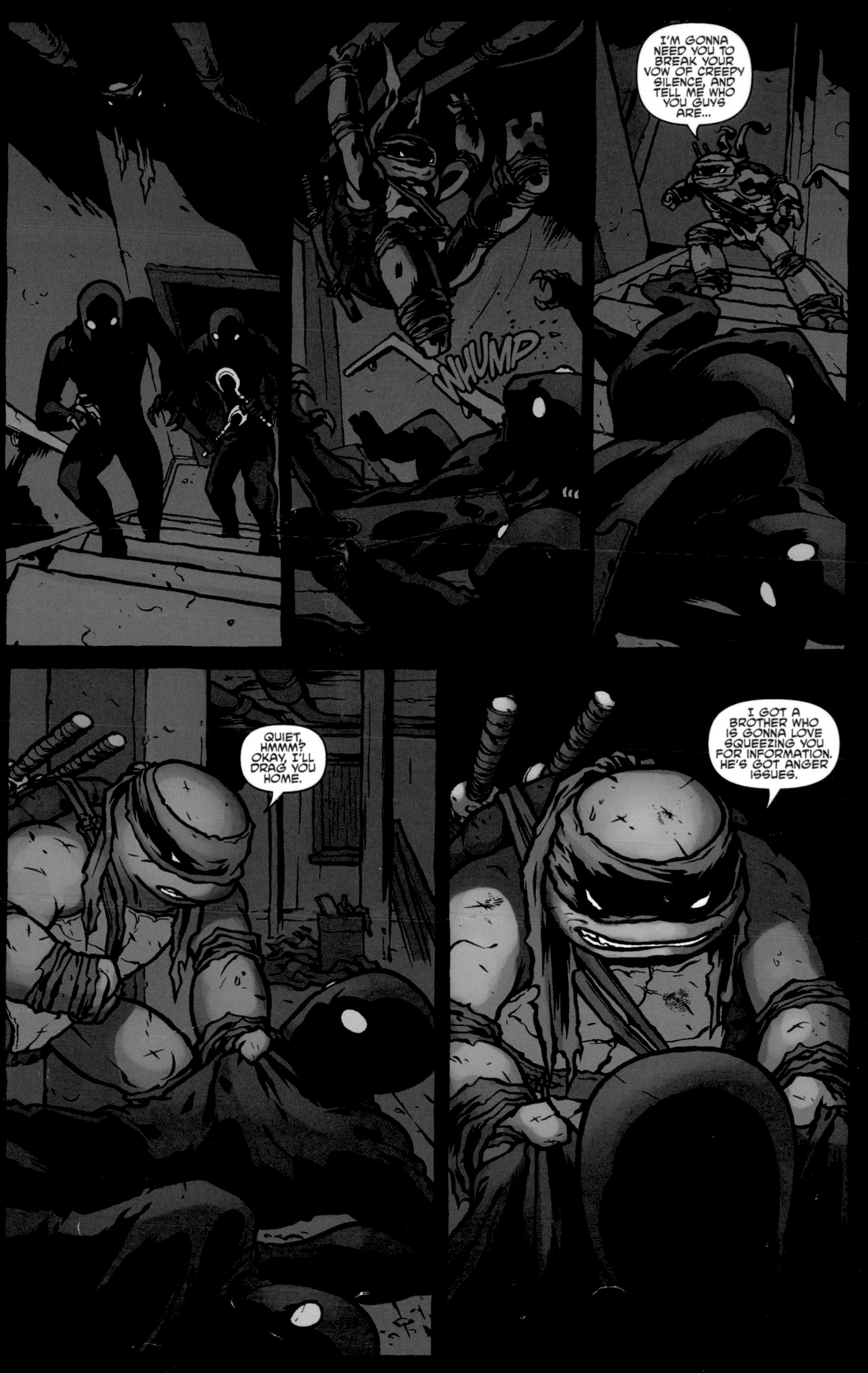
WHUMP
I'M GONNA NEED YOU TO BREAK YOUR VOW OF CREEPY SILENCE, AND TELL ME WHO YOU GUYS ARE...
QUIET, HMMM? OKAY, I'LL DRAG YOU HOME.
I GOT A BROTHER WHO IS GONNA LOVE SQUEEZING YOU FOR INFORMATION. HE'S GOT ANGER ISSUES.

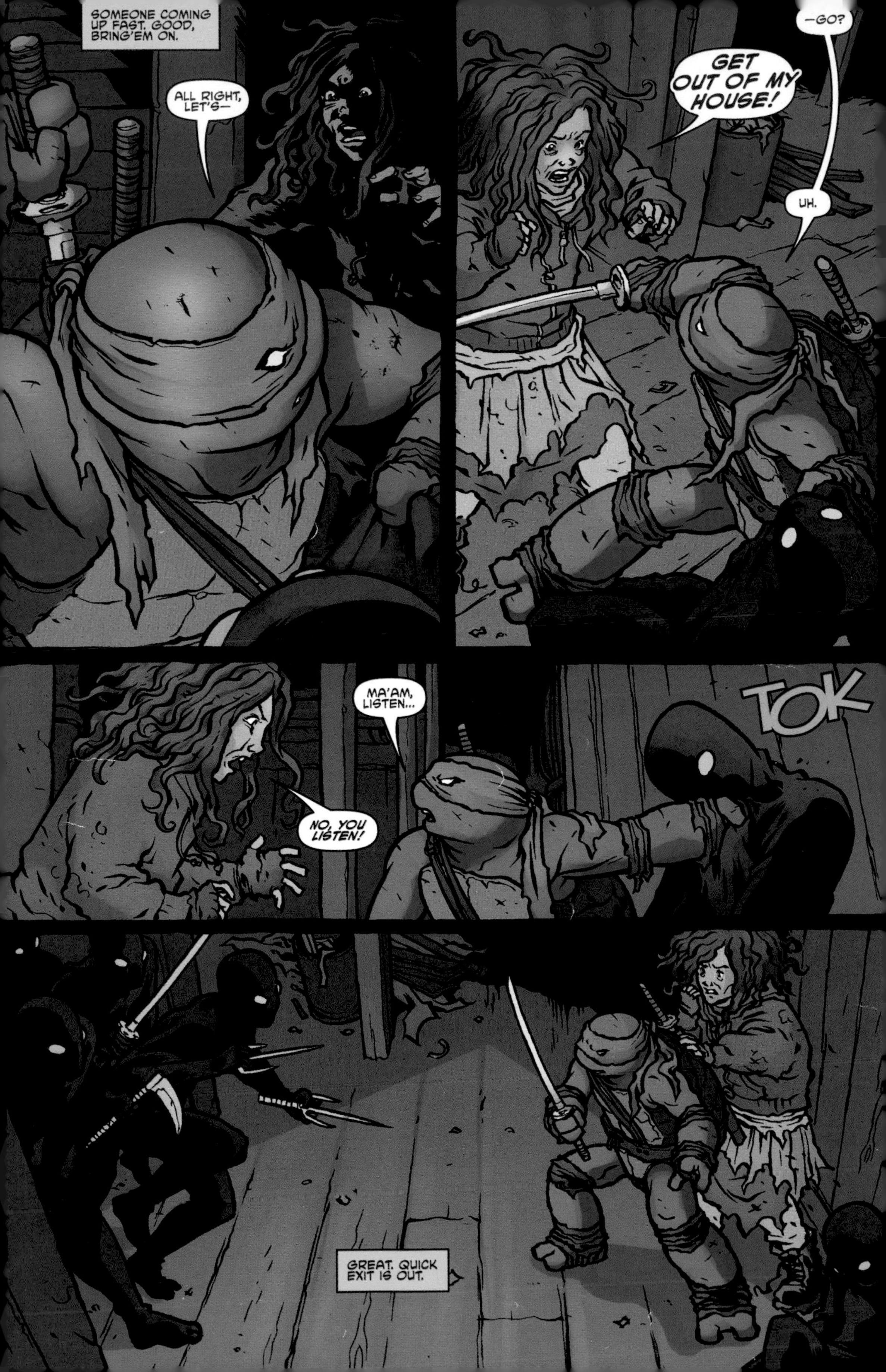
SOMEONE COMING UP FAST. GOOD, BRING'EM ON.
ALL RIGHT, LET'S—
GET OUT OF MY HOUSE!
—GO?
UH.
MA'AM, LISTEN...
NO, YOU LISTEN!
TOK
GREAT. QUICK EXIT IS OUT.

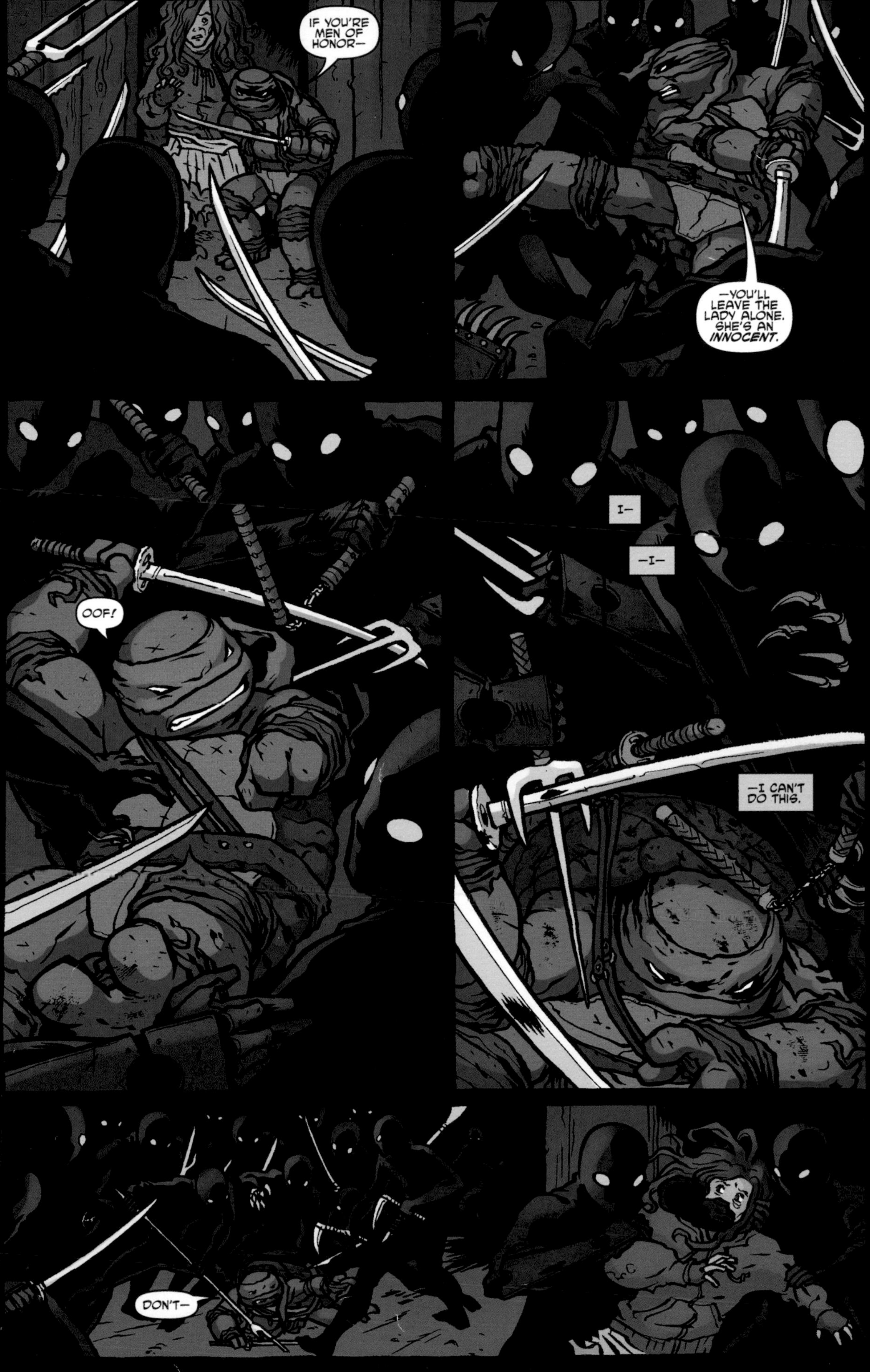
IF YOU'RE MEN OF HONOR—
—YOU'LL LEAVE THE LADY ALONE. SHE'S AN *INNOCENT*.
OOF!
I—
—I—
—I CAN'T DO THIS.
DON'T—

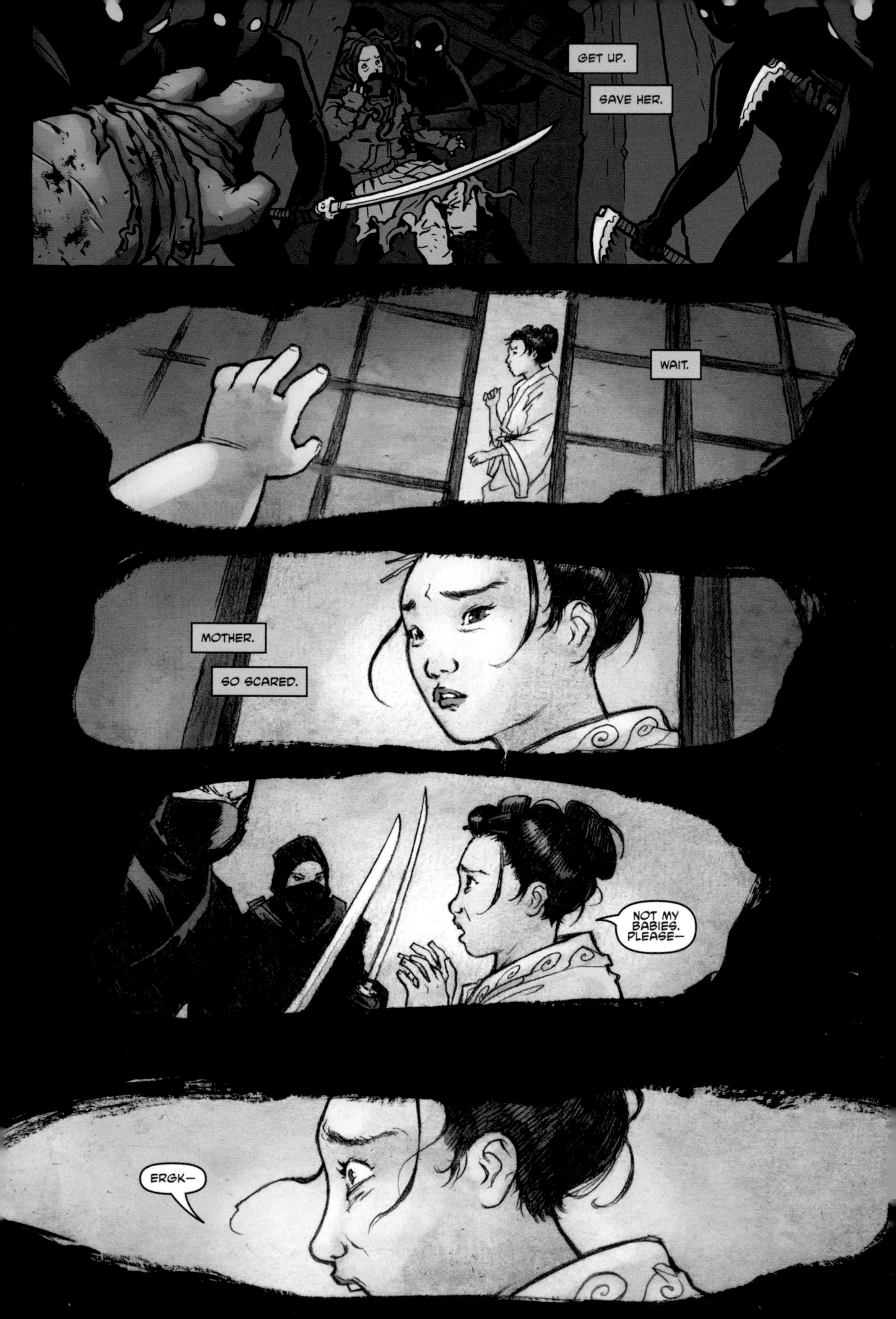
GET UP.
SAVE HER.
WAIT.
MOTHER.
SO SCARED.
NOT MY BABIES. PLEASE—
ERGK—

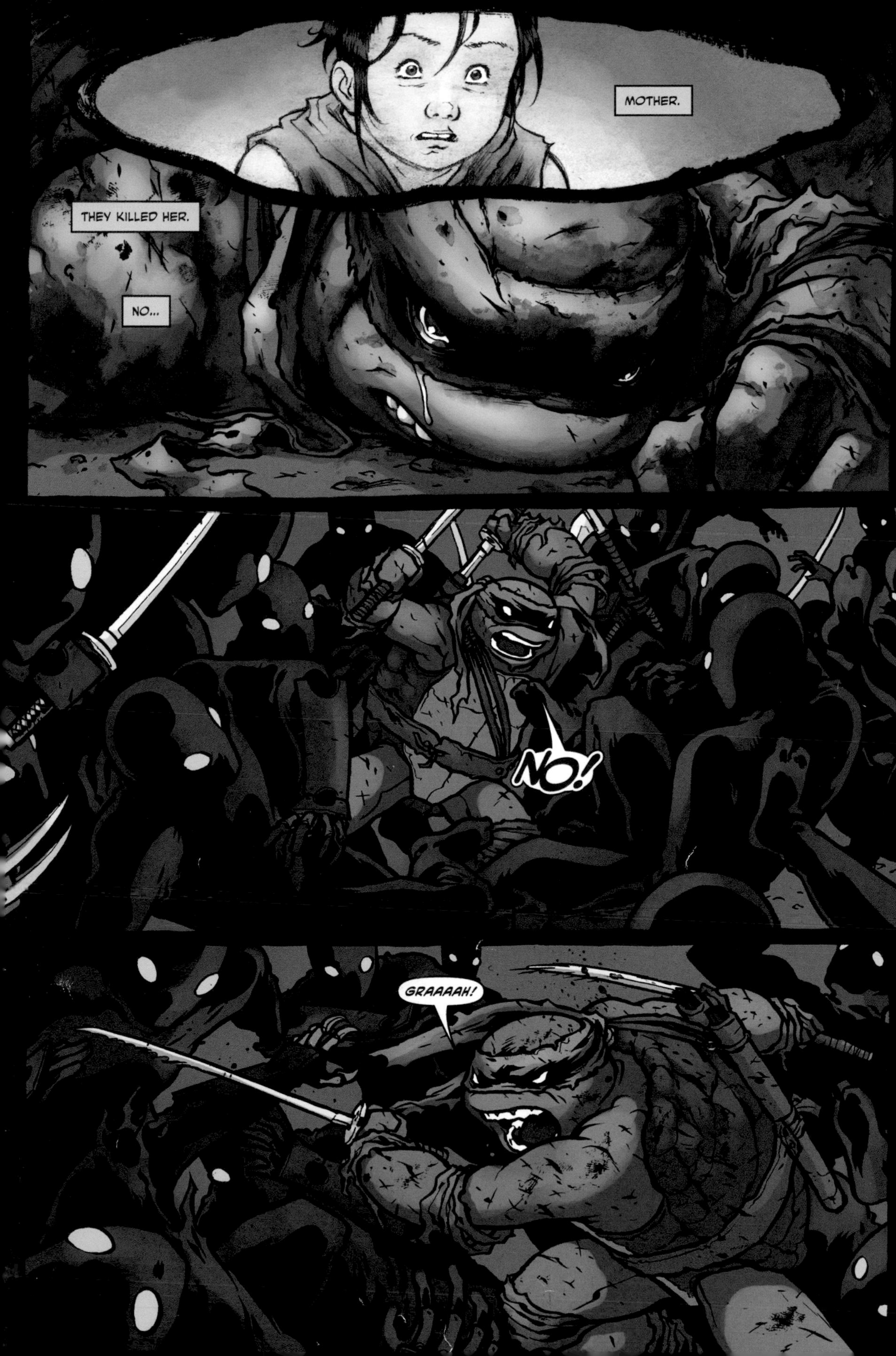
MOTHER.
THEY KILLED HER.
NO...
NO!
GRAAAAH!

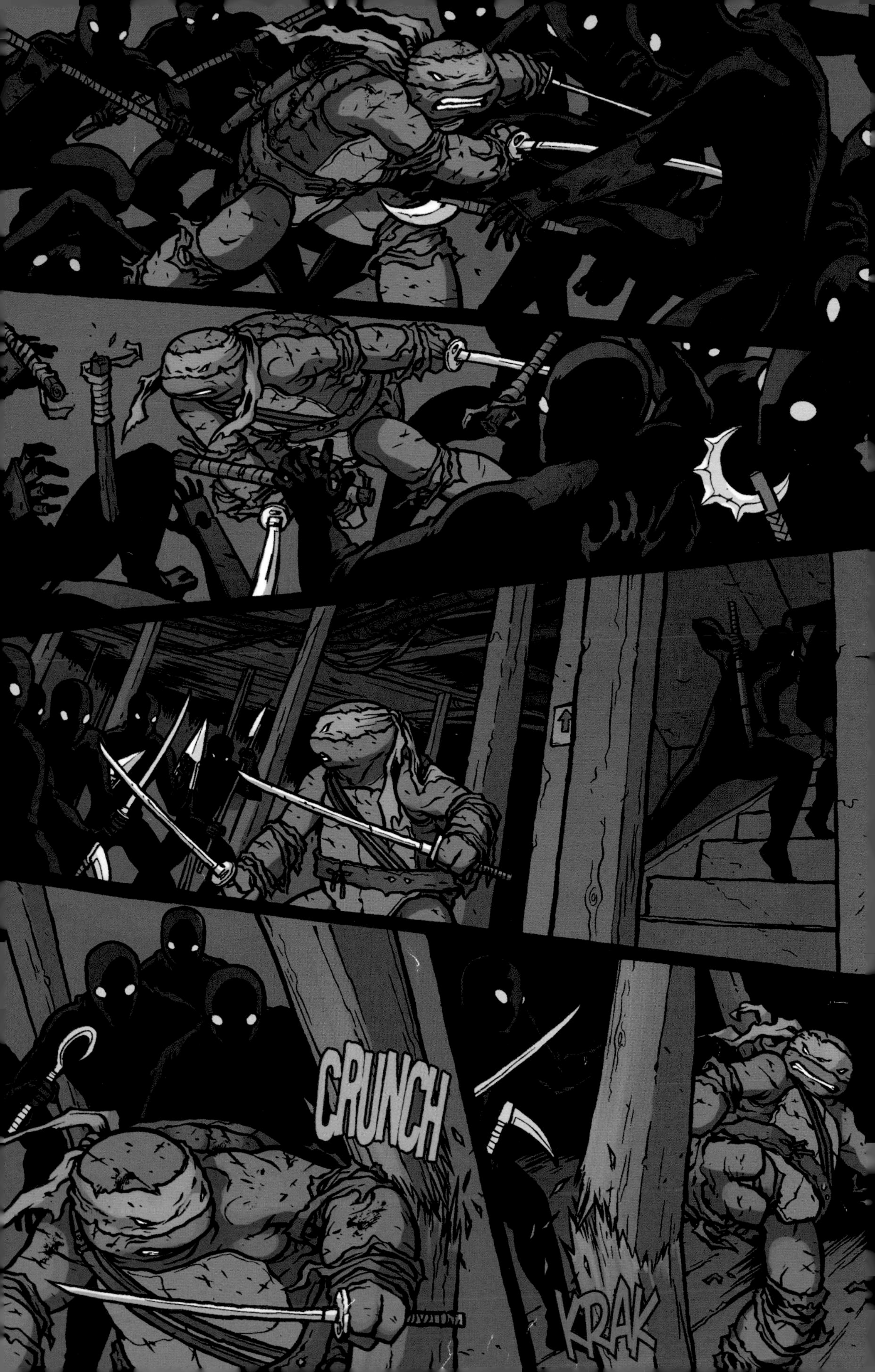
CRUNCH
KRAK

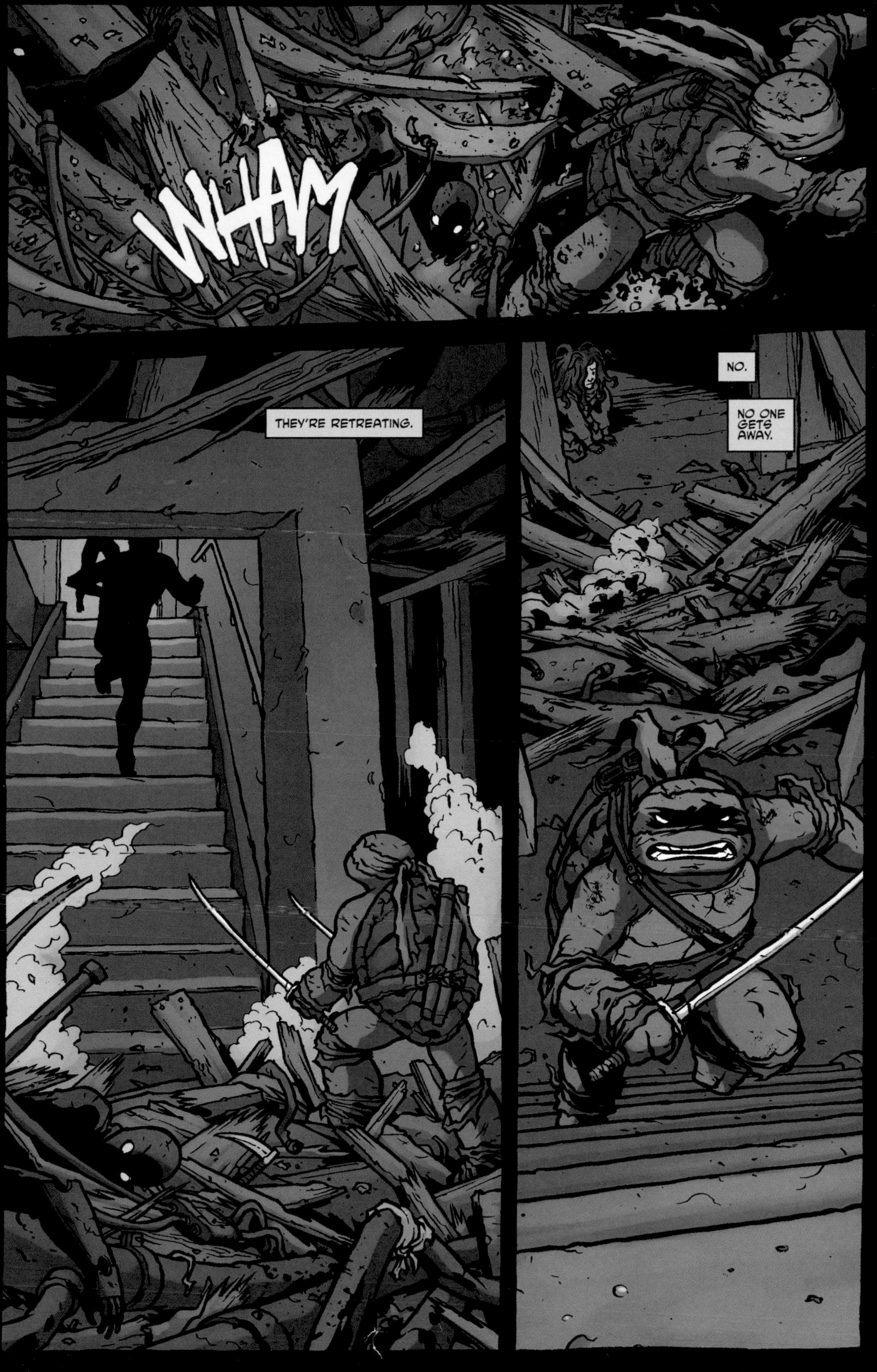
WHAM
THEY'RE RETREATING.
NO.
NO ONE GETS AWAY.

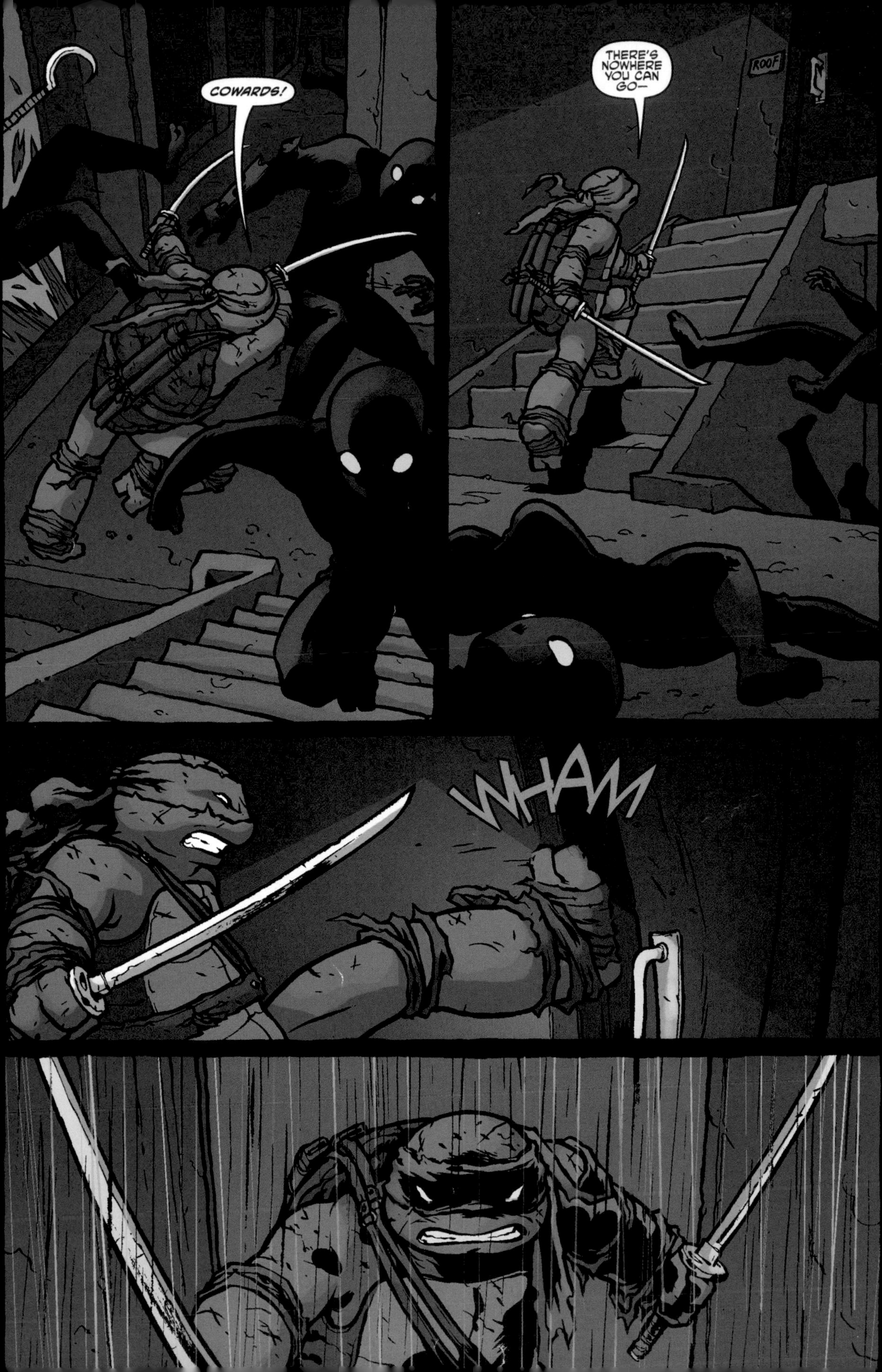
COWARDS!
THERE'S NOWHERE YOU CAN GO—
ROOF
WHAM

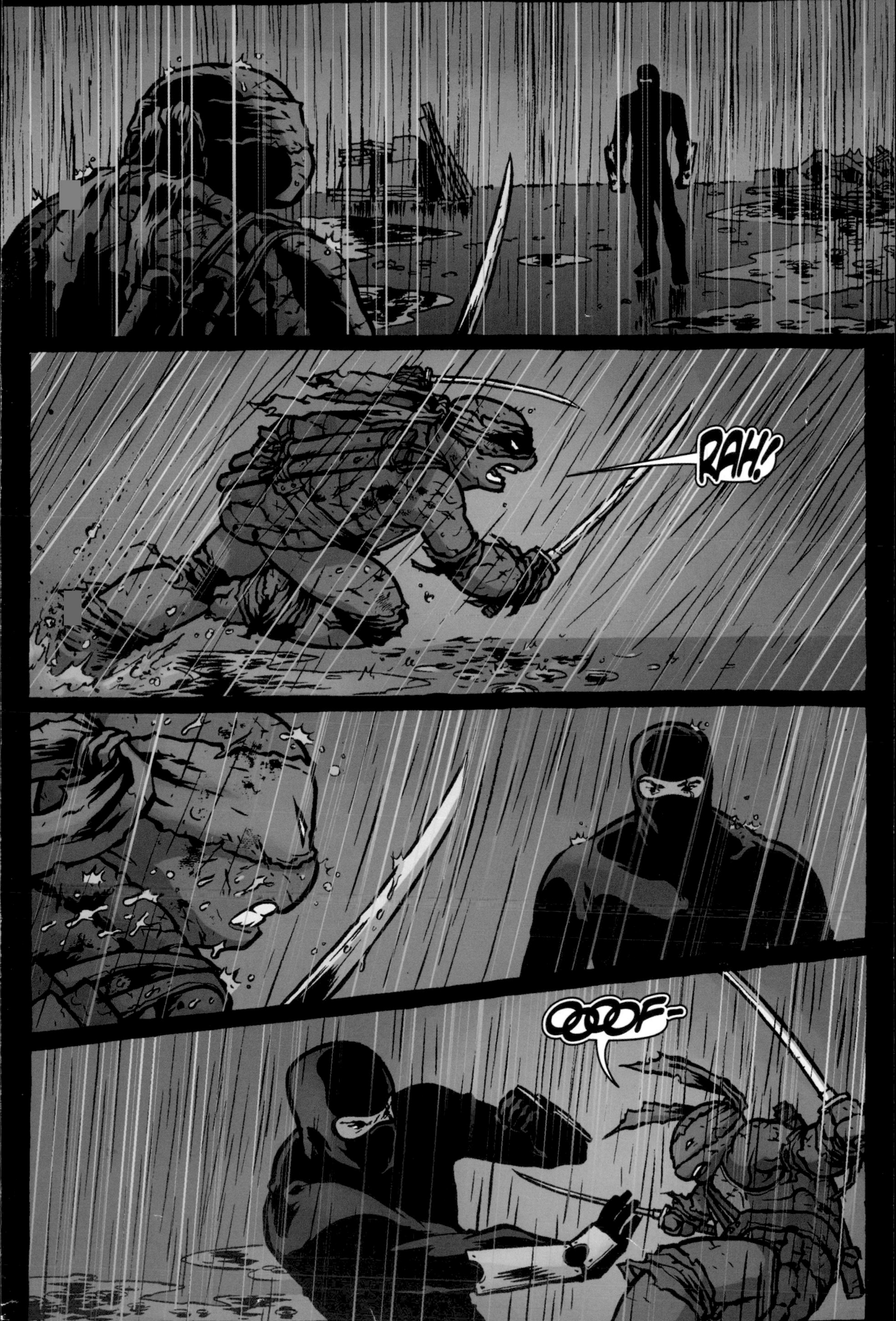
RAH!
OOOF-

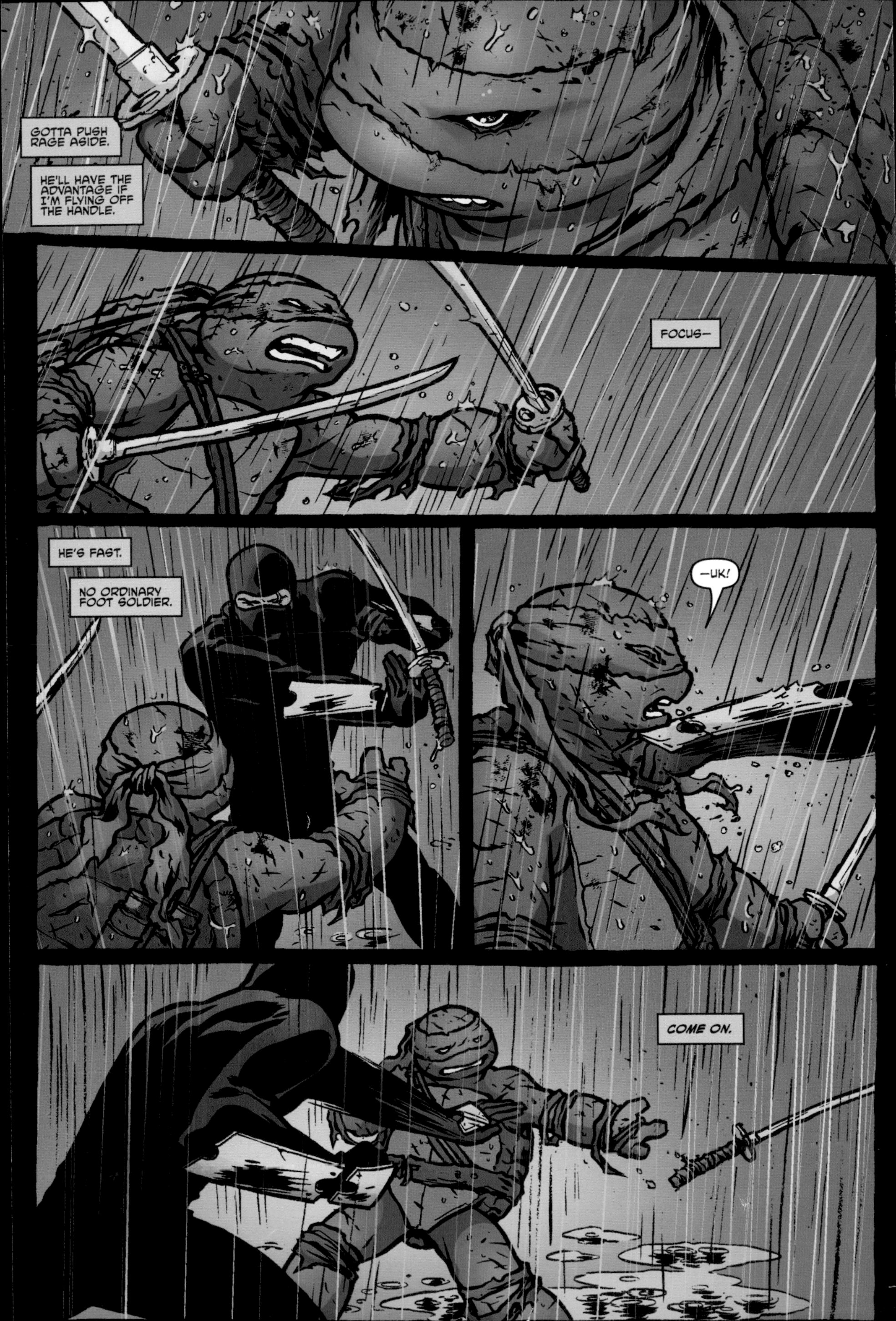
GOTTA PUSH RAGE ASIDE.
HE'LL HAVE THE ADVANTAGE IF I'M FLYING OFF THE HANDLE.
FOCUS—
HE'S FAST.
NO ORDINARY FOOT SOLDIER.
—UK!
COME ON.

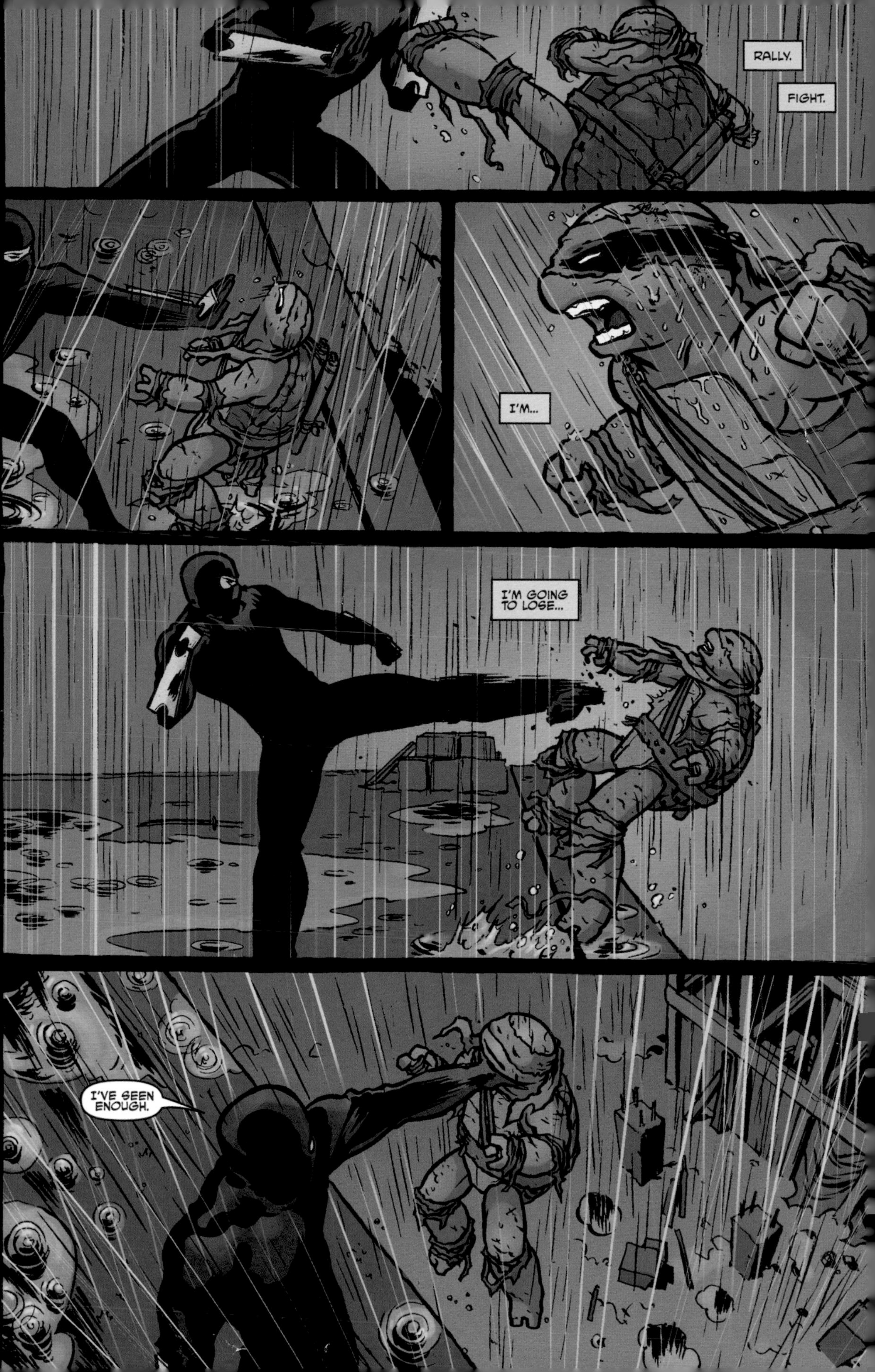
RALLY.
FIGHT.
I'M...
I'M GOING TO LOSE...
I'VE SEEN ENOUGH.

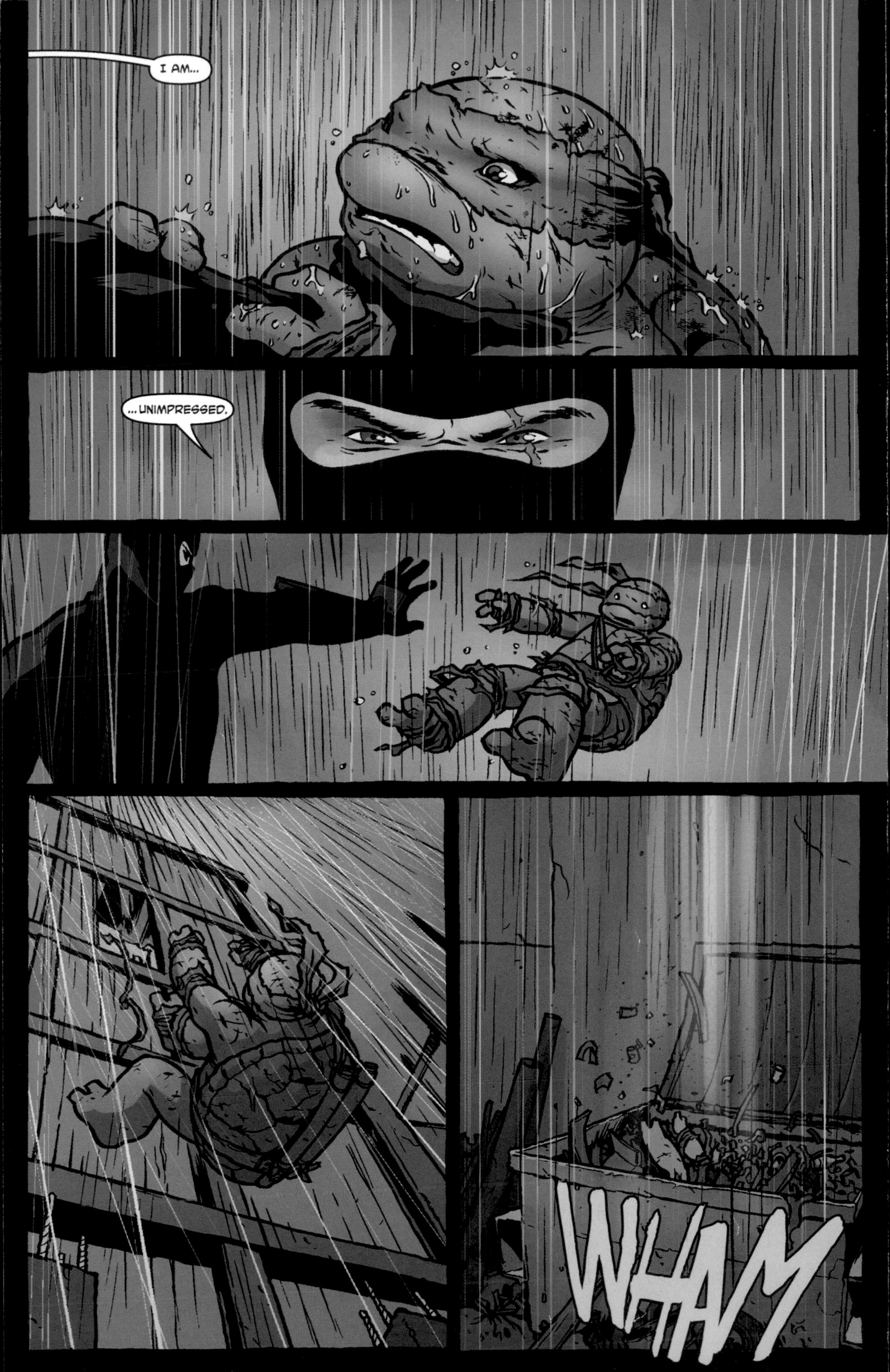
I AM...
...UNIMPRESSED.
WHAM

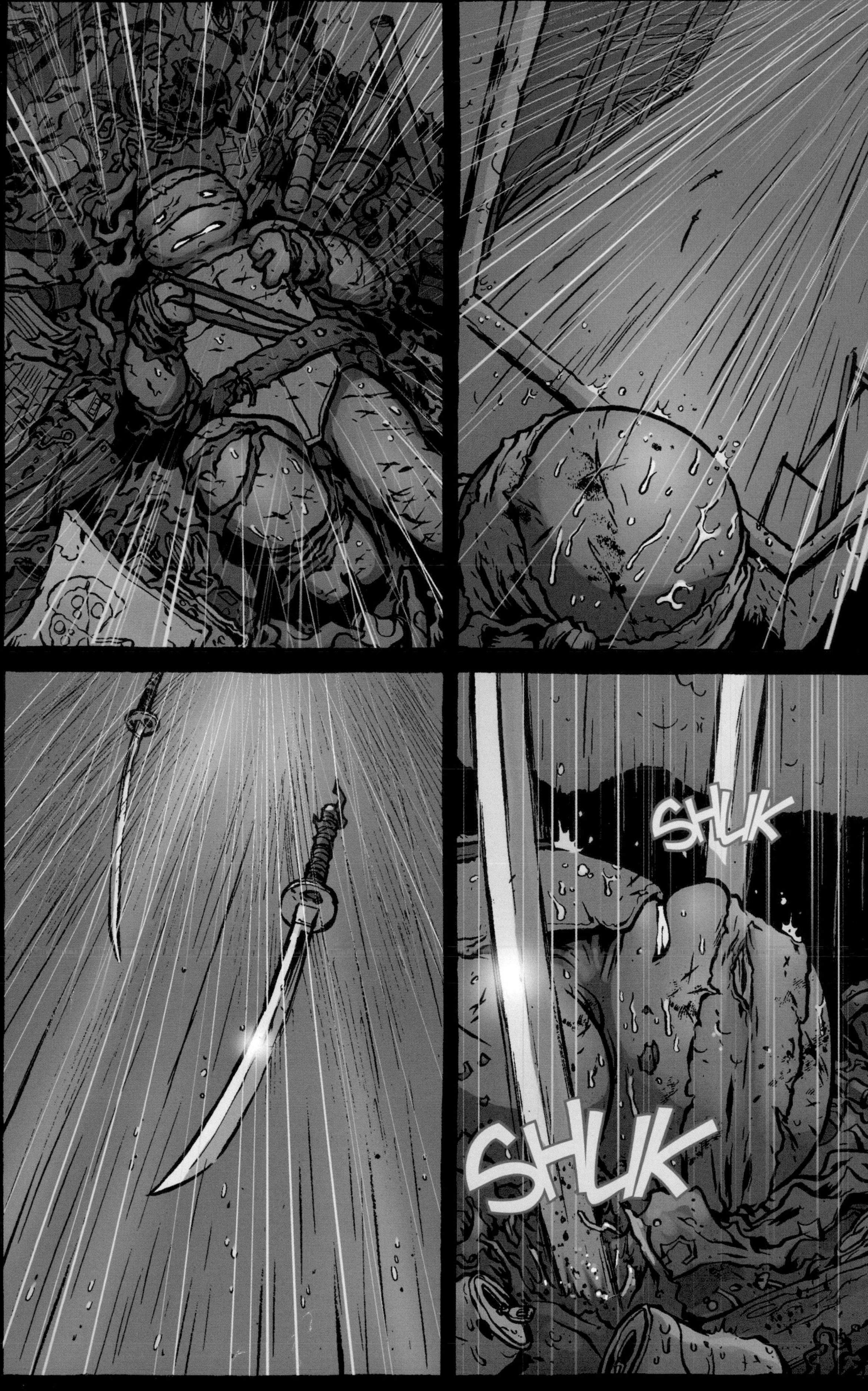
SHUK
SHUK

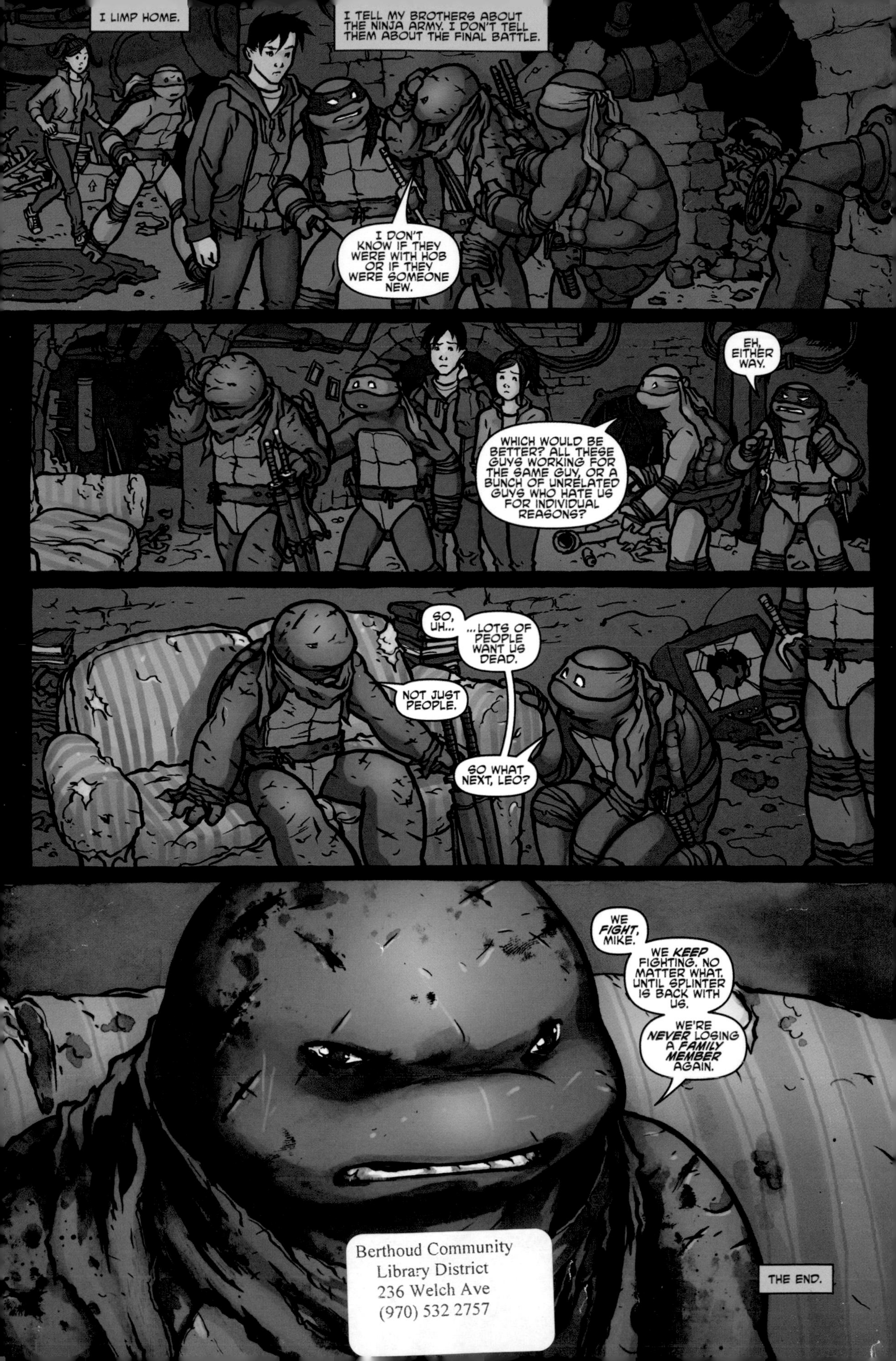
I LIMP HOME.
I TELL MY BROTHERS ABOUT THE NINJA ARMY. I DON'T TELL THEM ABOUT THE FINAL BATTLE.
I DON'T KNOW IF THEY WERE WITH HOB OR IF THEY WERE SOMEONE NEW.
EH, EITHER WAY.
WHICH WOULD BE BETTER? ALL THESE GUYS WORKING FOR THE SAME GUY, OR A BUNCH OF UNRELATED GUYS WHO HATE US FOR INDIVIDUAL REASONS?
SO, UH...
...LOTS OF PEOPLE WANT US DEAD.
NOT JUST PEOPLE.
SO WHAT NEXT, LEO?
WE FIGHT, MIKE.
WE KEEP FIGHTING. NO MATTER WHAT. UNTIL SPLINTER IS BACK WITH US.
WE'RE NEVER LOSING A FAMILY MEMBER AGAIN.
THE END.